THE SECRETS OF DROON

Search for the Dragon Ship

by Tony Abbott

Illustrated by Tim Jessell

A
LITTLE APPLE
PAPERBACK

SCHOLASTIC INC.
New York Toronto London Auckland Sydney
Mexico City New Delhi Hong Kong Buenos Aires

For Rob Boyd
and Amanda Barrett,
friends extraordinaire

For more information about the continuing saga of Droon,
please visit Tony Abbott's website at
www.tonyabbottbooks.com

Book design by Dawn Adelman

ISBN 0-439-42079-2

12   7 8/0

Printed in the U.S.A.   40
First printing, May 2003

Contents

1. A Kick from Beyond   1

2. The Not-nice Princess   15

3. The Hands of Thog   27

4. Eyes in the Darkness   38

5. Surprise by Candlelight   48

6. Island of Secrets   60

7. The Puzzle of the Past   72

8. Zello's Believe It or Not   85

9. A Very Important Person   100

10. Follow That Ship!   109

One

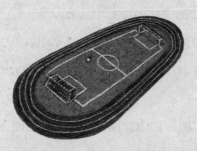

A Kick from Beyond

"Slow down!" said Eric Hinkle as he and his friend Julie raced around the track behind school.

It was Field Day, and their class was outside shooting hoops, playing catch, jumping, swinging, climbing, and running.

Eric glanced down at Julie's feet.

Well, at least *he* was running.

"Someone will see you," Eric huffed.

"But it's so much fun!" said Julie, pumping her arms and legs as if she were running fast.

She wasn't running. Her feet never touched the ground. Julie was flying.

Eric hustled to keep up with her. "Having powers is fun, but you have to keep them a secret —"

"See ya!" said Julie, zipping away and leaving him in the dust.

"We need to keep *you-know-where* a secret, too!" Eric called out as he slowed to a jog.

Julie knew where. So did their friend Neal.

The place to keep secret was Droon.

Droon was the strange land they had discovered one day under Eric's basement.

It was a world filled with wonderful friends, like the great and powerful Galen Longbeard, and Keeah, a young wizard and princess, and Max, a furry little eight-legged spider troll.

Droon was also a land of mystery and magic.

In fact, it was on the kids' last adventure there that Julie was scratched by an ancient magical creature called a wingwolf.

Eric remembered the prophecy he'd been told.

The one who strikes the wolf at noon, shall earn a secret wish in Droon.

Julie's secret wish, she told Eric and Neal later, had always been to fly. And thanks to her battle with the wingwolf, now she could.

Still pretending to run, Julie flew around the track to where Neal was dribbling a soccer ball.

Eric walked across the field to them.

"Julie, that was so awesome!" said Neal.

She laughed. "Last night I flew out over my backyard. I almost fell, but I keep surprising myself. On the stairs at home, playing hoops — it's just so easy to take off and start flying —"

"And easy to be caught," said Eric with a frown. "And besides, you never know if the wingwolf gave you other powers you don't know about."

He didn't want to sound like a big brother, but he knew that powers had a way of coming out when you least expected them to.

"Sorry," said Julie. "I guess I should be nervous. But I always wanted to fly. You already have powers. This is really new to me."

That was true. Eric had had powers

ever since he was accidentally zapped by Keeah's magic. He couldn't control them all, but he hoped he was getting better at it.

"Anyway," said Neal, "with crazy Salamandra on the loose in Droon, we should probably train as much as we can, right?"

They shuddered to recall the name.

Salamandra, Princess of Shadowthorn.

Traveling through time in the Upper World, Salamandra had stolen magic from the greatest wizards of the past. She had become very powerful. Now she was in Droon.

"I can't fly or shoot sparks," said Neal. "But watch this." He began bouncing a soccer ball on his head. *Boing!* "Ouch!" *Boing!* "Ouch!" *Boing!* "Ouch! Pretty — ouch! — cool, huh?"

"Doesn't it hurt your head?" asked Eric.

Neal shrugged. "No more than math class."

Weeeee! Mr. Frando, the gym coach, blew his whistle. "Last event of the day, kids," he announced. "The soccer kick! Bring all the balls in."

As Neal rounded up the balls he'd been using, there was a sudden whooshing sound overhead.

The three friends looked up to see a soccer ball in mid-flight, zigzagging across the field. It dipped sharply, circled their heads, then arched up and plopped down onto the school roof.

Eric turned to Neal. "How did you —"

"I didn't," he said. "I don't have powers."

"But that ball does," said Julie. "It's like . . ."

Eric gasped. "Whoa! You don't think it's *our* soccer ball, do you? The one that Keeah put her magic spell on?"

Long ago, after their first visit to Droon, Keeah had enchanted the kids' soccer ball to give them messages whenever they were needed in Droon.

"If it is our soccer ball," said Neal, "how are we going to get up to the school roof?"

Julie grinned. "Create a distraction. I'll fly up!"

"A distraction?" said Neal, his face lighting up. "You've come to the right guy. Watch this!"

Neal grabbed a soccer ball, started bouncing it on his head, and ran onto the field, yelling, "Blaga-blaga-yee-yee-yee! Go-team-go!"

Everyone stared at him, then started laughing.

Even Mr. Frando laughed. "Neal, you're a nut! But full of spirit. Everyone — yell like Neal!"

While the whole class was yelling and chasing Neal around the field, Julie leaped up.

As if she had invisible wings, she fluttered all the way up to the school roof.

Eric checked the field. No one had seen her.

A moment later, she leaned over the edge. "Eric, get up here right away! Find Neal, too!"

While the other kids gathered for the last event, Eric waved Neal over. They both slipped into the school and charged up the stairs to the roof.

Julie called them over. "Take a look at this."

Holding the ball in front of her, she let it go. But the ball didn't drop. It hovered in the air.

"Whoa!" said Neal. "It *is* our magic ball. Do you think someone is calling us to Droon?"

All of a sudden, the ball's white and

black patches began to shift, moving across the surface until the ball was entirely black.

Eric shivered. "This doesn't look good."

"You think it has something to do with Salamandra?" asked Julie.

Before anyone could answer, letters appeared on the ball, as if written by an invisible hand.

$$G \ldots A \ldots L \ldots E \ldots N$$

Eric staggered back. "Oh, my gosh. Galen's trying to send us a message. What is it? What?"

But as quickly as they had appeared, the letters vanished. Then the ball dropped, bounced, and lay still, a normal soccer ball once more.

Julie snatched it up. "This means one thing, at least. We have to get to Droon now."

They hustled down the stairs and out to the field just in time to hear Coach Frando's whistle marking the end of the last event.

A moment later, the dismissal bell rang.

"I can't believe we missed the soccer kick," Neal grumbled.

Eric smiled. "Maybe we'll have a chance to kick Salamandra out of Droon. Let's go."

The three friends ran for their bus. Twenty minutes later, they raced across Eric's front yard, burst through the kitchen, and tramped down to his basement.

Julie set the enchanted soccer ball on the workbench, while Neal and Eric pulled two heavy cartons away from a small door under the stairs.

Beyond the door was a tiny room, empty except for a lightbulb hanging from the low ceiling.

They crowded in. Neal switched on the light.

"No matter how many times we do this," said Julie, "it still gives me chills."

"Me, too," said Neal. "Every time."

Eric grinned. "Ditto for me."

He shut the door and switched off the light.

The room went dark for a moment, then — *whoosh!* — the floor disappeared. In its place, shimmering in its own bright light, was a set of stairs curving down and away from the house.

Eric took the first step. "I hope Galen's not in trouble or anything. We'd better hurry."

Step-by-step, the kids descended through pink clouds, until they found themselves above a desert of rolling sand dunes.

But the normally bright sky over the dunes was streaked with smoke.

Julie frowned. "What's going on here?"

"It looks like Lumpland," said Neal, "home of Khan and the Lumpies — whoa — look at that!"

Nestled between a large dune and a small village of mud houses, was a stone tower.

They had seen it before in different parts of Droon. It was Galen's enchanted traveling tower.

And there, pacing in a circle around the base of the tower, her hair a long cascade of prickly thorns, her skin purple and scaly, was the wicked sorceress herself.

Salamandra, Princess of Shadowthorn.

"It's her," said Julie. "And she looks mad."

"Is she ever anything else?" asked Neal.

In her hand, Salamandra held a tall wooden staff. At its tip, a cluster of pointed thorns burned with a violent green flame.

"Wizard, give me what I seek!" Salamandra shouted, her catlike eyes gleaming yellow. "You know where it is — I want it now!"

Galen appeared at the tower's upper window. His face looked stern. "Never!" he shouted.

"That's right — never!" chirped his spider troll friend, Max, trembling next to him.

Salamandra narrowed her eyes. "Then prepare for a fight!" She aimed her staff, and a blast of flaming thorns shot up through the air.

"Holy cow!" gasped Eric.

Vvvv-boom! The thorns struck the tower, rocking it back and forth in the sand.

"Oh!" cried Max. "Oh, dear — help!"

Two

The Not-nice Princess

Vvvv-boom! Vvvv-boom! — Salamandra hurled more flaming thorns at the tower.

"Don't make me come up there!" she yelled.

"Y-y-you s-s-stop that!" cried a lumpy pillow-shaped creature charging up from the village. He wagged a short wooden sword at Salamandra.

"It's Khan, king of the Lumpies!" said Julie. "Khan, watch out! She's a meanie —"

"What? Oh!" The tiny king leaped back to his little mud house just as — *vvvv-boom!* — thorns exploded right where he had been standing.

As the wicked princess turned her attention back to Galen's tower, the kids scrambled down the dune to Khan's house, where the Lumpy king and his family were huddled inside.

"Are you all right?" asked Eric.

"It's terrible," said Khan, shaking sand from his shoulder tassels. "She just appeared from nowhere and attacked Galen's tower. We barely escaped!"

Cuddling their two Lumpy children, Mrs. Khan continued, "Keeah is trying to get into the tower. But the poor dear hasn't had any luck —"

Boom! A blast rocked the house at the

exact moment a girl in a blue tunic flew in the front door. "Well, that didn't work!" she said.

"Keeah!" said Julie. "Are you all right?"

The princess of Droon smiled to see her friends. "So far," she said. "Galen and Max are fighting back, but I haven't gotten close yet."

"I am ready to serve," said Khan, holding up his little sword again. "I can give you cover."

Mrs. Khan looked worriedly at him. So did the children, their pillowy faces wrinkling with fear.

"We'll help Keeah on this one, Khan," said Eric. "You should probably stay here to protect your family until Salamandra's gone."

Khan sheathed his sword. "Right you are," he said. "But call me the moment things get rough."

"We will," said Keeah. "Is everyone ready?"

Neal nodded. "You bet. Let's mess up Little Miss Tangle Hair's plans. Whatever they are!"

The four friends crept carefully out the door. At once, Salamandra threw a blast. *Vvvv-boom!*

"That happens every time I try to get close!" said Keeah, leaping behind a sand dune.

"What if we fly up to the tower?" asked Julie. Then she told Keeah about what had been happening since the wingwolf scratched her. "It's totally healed. But now I can fly. Cool, huh?"

"She's pretty good at it already," said Neal.

Keeah blinked. "Let's try it. Come on."

While Salamandra was busy conjuring more flaming blasts, Julie held out her hands, everyone grabbed on, and — *fwit-fwit!* — she fluttered up to the topmost room of the tower.

Blam! Blam! Galen was at the far window, hurling blue thunderbolts at Salamandra while Max scrambled around searching through books.

"A spell, a spell!" he chittered. "We must find a spell! That terrible creature is after something!"

"What's going on?" asked Keeah.

Galen's eyes flashed with anger. "Salamandra has been up to her old tricks, stealing magic —"

"And our secret thoughts, too," said Max. "It's as if she can read our minds!"

Ka-foom! The tower wobbled in the sand and suddenly — *blam!*— the door blew wide open.

And Salamandra stormed into the room.

"Sorry to barge in," she snarled. "But I couldn't wait for you to invite me."

Both Keeah and Galen leveled blasts of blue lightning at her, but the princess simply thrust out her staff and their lightning vanished into it.

Then she lifted her hand and — *flang* — everyone seemed rooted to where they stood.

Eric tried to raise his hand to blast her, but found he couldn't move. "I'm . . . stuck!"

"I stole that little trick from an old witch," the thorn princess said, the flames on her staff sizzling as she gazed deeply into their eyes.

Eric recalled Salamandra's amazing power to reach into the deepest parts of people's minds and discover their secrets. It was like being hypnotized.

"Pah," she snarled. "You cannot help me!"

"As if we'd want to," snapped Neal.

She then pointed a long purple finger at Max. "You! Furry one! You know what I want —"

"We know what you need," Julie mumbled. "A complete makeover!"

Salamandra flicked her staff and a sharp green light shot out, encircling Max's head. His eyes lit up with the same green light and began to roll. An instant later, he clambered up to the room's highest shelf and pulled down a folded paper.

A cruel smile broke over the sorceress's face as she snatched the paper and unfolded it. "So the legends are true. How very . . . perfect. . . ."

"How very wicked, you mean," said Keeah.

"Thorn princess, you don't know what you are doing," said Galen, his eyes flashing. "Where you seek to go is a place of darkness and evil."

Salamandra stared at the wizard. "Just the way I like it. See you later, old man!"

With that, she leaped to the window and — *ka-foom!* — vanished from sight.

Max whimpered. "Oh, I'm so . . . sorry. . . ."

"Do not blame yourself, my friend," said Galen, patting Max on the head. "Her power is nearly impossible to fight."

"What is on the paper?" asked Keeah.

Galen took a deep breath. "A picture I drew long ago. It shows a ship . . . a *flying* ship —"

"In the shape of a dragon!" chirped Max. "Built by the evil Emperor Ko centuries ago. Salamandra wants to find it — and fly it —"

Vvvv-booom! A sudden spray of thorns

blasted through the upper window, struck the wall, and began to grow and spread around the room.

"Oh, my gosh," said Keeah. "Everyone out!"

But the instant the kids jumped through the door and into the hallway, thorns coiled around it, blocking the way.

"Galen and Max are still inside," cried Julie. "They'll be trapped —"

Keeah and Eric shot at the thorns, but their blasts only made the thorns grow more quickly.

"Wicked curse," Galen called out from behind the door. "Go — stop her — stop her —"

Thorns began to slither up the walls.

"We'll be trapped, too," said Neal. "Hurry!"

The kids raced down through the tower and tumbled outside, only to find thorns growing over the entire tower. The wizard's home was barely visible.

"Galen!" cried Eric. "Can you hear us¿"

A faint call came from the window. "Thog!"

Eric turned to Keeah. "Did he say *thog*¿"

"It sounded like *thog*," said the princess.

"Maybe it means good luck," said Julie.

"Thog to you, too!" yelled Neal.

"No!" cried Max. "Find Thog! Salamandra will seek him out. Find him first! At Zorfendorf!"

Then a large sheet of paper fluttered down from the tower's upper window.

Julie caught it, then looked at her friends. "It's a map of Droon. I guess we're on a treasure hunt."

Khan scurried up a dune to them. "And we must start now. Come, my pilkas can take us to Zorfendorf."

Keeah stared at the tower. "Galen!" she called out. "We'll stop Salamandra!" Then under her breath, she murmured, "Somehow . . ."

Mrs. Khan and her children quickly brought the pilkas. She hugged the king, saying, "Be very careful, dear. And hurry back."

"I shall return by suppertime," said Khan.

The shaggy, six-legged beasts whinnied — *hrrr!* — the kids piled on, and — *wumpeta-wumpeta!* — they galloped away swiftly.

Behind them, the wizard's tower grew black with thorns, and the voices of Galen and Max became too faint to hear.

Three

The Hands of Thog

Wumpeta-wumpeta! The shaggy pilkas galloped south across the dunes, carrying the children to Zorfendorf Castle.

"If we hurry," said Khan, "we'll get there before the wicked princess."

Julie made a face. "Princess? Ha! She doesn't even deserve the name!"

Eric wondered what Salamandra was really up to. Why did she want a flying ship? She was already so powerful. What more could she want? Would they find out before it was too late? And, most important, could they stop her?

He looked over at his friends riding their pilkas at top speed. He smiled. As long as they stuck together, things just might turn out okay.

"Look," said Keeah, pointing to the red-topped towers of a castle rising on a distant hill. "Zorfendorf Castle. And not a single thorn on it. We're in time."

They rode quickly to the old castle. When the guards saw Keeah, they opened the gate wide.

The chief guard bowed as they entered. "Prince Zorfendorf is not here now, but we are always happy when our princess visits," he said.

"Yeah, well, another princess is coming," said Neal. "And you won't be so happy to see her!"

The children explained what had happened and that they were actually there to see Thog.

"Thog?" The chief guard blinked. "But he hasn't left the library since he came here!"

"How long has he been here?" asked Julie.

"Four hundred years!" said the guard.

Eric frowned. "We still need to see him."

"In the meantime, prepare for an attack," said Khan, tapping his little sword. "Salamandra is coming. And she's angry."

"Plus, don't look at that weird staff she carries," said Neal. "She'll take over your brain."

As the guards piled ten-deep at the castle gate and along the upper walls, the children hurried through one hallway, up a narrow staircase, down a wide one, around seven corners, and into a long tunnel.

"No wonder Thog never leaves the library," said Neal. "He probably can't find his way out."

Khan chuckled. "I smell books up ahead."

After two more turns and one more set of stairs, they came upon a room the size of a school gym. From floor to ceiling were shelves holding thousands and thousands of books, their gold, red, and blue covers gleaming brightly.

"Big library," said Eric, peering up.

Julie beamed. "What beautiful books!" She fluttered up to one of the high shelves to look.

"The prince collects them," said a low voice.

The children turned to see a shelf move aside. Out of the darkness behind it, stepped . . .

"Holy cow — a giant!" gasped Neal.

Thog was as tall as a two-story house. The three floppy ears on his bald head brushed the ceiling as he entered. A fur wrap hung from his shoulders to his knees. His belt was made of thick rope.

He gazed at the children with big round eyes. "Visitors? Come to see me?"

Keeah bowed. "Galen sent us to find you, sir."

"Galen?" Thog put a large hand to his mouth to cover his toothy smile. "The good wizard Galen sent you? Oh, how is the dear man?"

"Not so good at the moment," said Eric.

Thog's large face changed from wonder to worry as he listened to the story of Salamandra and her attack on Galen's tower.

For a while he said nothing. Finally, he sighed. "Long ago, when we were both young, Galen let me borrow a book. This book!"

He took a slender yellow volume from a shelf and handed it to Julie. "Do you like books?"

"Very much," she said.

Thog smiled. "Then you may borrow it, too. Because of Galen's kindness, I learned to love books. In thanks, I helped him hide something."

Eric glanced at Keeah, then back up at Thog. "By any chance did you hide . . . a flying ship?"

Thog trembled, then nodded. "Four hundred years ago, Galen found an evil dragon ship. He tried to destroy it, but its magic was too old. So he took it apart, and together we hid the pieces. So that it could never be flown again. . . ."

Neal raised his hand. "I don't get it. Salamandra already does pretty much what she wants. Why does she need a ship that flies around?"

"Maybe because of where this ship flies to," said Thog. "But, oh . . . I've said too much."

There was a sudden cry from outside, and a flash of green light shot past the upper window.

"Don't say any more," said Julie flying down from the top shelf. "Don't *think* it. She's here!"

"What about the guards?" said Neal.

Wham! The door swung open with a bang. Salamandra strode in, her staff burning bright.

"You don't believe in knocking, do you?" said Keeah, her fingers glowing with bright sparks.

"Not really," said Salamandra. Then, just as she had done in Galen's tower, she froze everyone right where they stood. Turning, she shot a sizzling beam of green light into Thog's eyes.

"Giant, you will take me to the dragon ship!"

He wobbled on his big feet. "Oh, no. My hands were made for reading books. This is my home. I can't leave here. . . . I . . . I . . ."

Even as he tried to fight it, the light penetrated his big round eyes. "I will lead you to the ship," he whispered.

Salamandra grinned. "There, was that so hard? Come, Thog. We have a journey to make!"

Laughing cruelly, Salamandra marched through the door again, the beams of her staff pulling Thog behind her like a pet.

The giant looked back at the children, his lips silently forming the words, "I'm . . . sorry. . . ."

"It's not your fault," Keeah called.

"After her!" said Eric as the green light faded and they could move again.

They dashed through the castle hallways and stairs. When they got to the front gate, the guards were bowing as Salamandra stormed out.

Khan grumbled. "Excuse me, guards, but whatever happened to *not* looking in her eyes?"

"Ha! No one resists my power!" Salamandra snarled. "And to prove it, say hello to some friends from ancient Droon. . . ."

Then, with a wave of her hand — *whoompf!* — a thick gray fog suddenly appeared on the plain outside the castle. She spat out the words of a spell, then she and Thog vanished.

"What did she say?" asked Neal. "It sounded like . . . 'toast biters.'"

The fog rolled closer, and a sound within it rumbled across the ground.

"Guys," said Eric, peering into the fog. "I'm not sure what Salamandra said, but

I'm pretty sure it had nothing to do with toast."

"I hear hooves," said Khan.

"Lots of them," said Julie.

Keeah gasped. "Ghost riders! Not toast biters — ghost riders!"

Neal frowned as the hooves stomped louder. "Ghost riders is not as good as toast. I like toast."

"There's a forest there," said Khan, pointing to a dark mass of trees behind the castle. "Leave the pilkas. We can hide better if we go on foot."

"I agree!" said Keeah. "But we must hurry —"

"Hurry fast!" added Julie.

The friends raced to the forest, as the strange dark fog rolled closer, and the sound of hooves thundered louder and louder.

Four

Eyes in the Darkness

Eric and Keeah crashed into the dark woods. Khan, Julie, and Neal hurried right behind.

Tangled branches clawed at them and jagged rocks cluttered the path as they stumbled to escape the ghost riders.

But the sound of bushes being ripped up and branches being torn down told them that the riders would stop at nothing to find them.

"What *are* ghost riders, anyway?" asked Neal. "And why don't they like us?"

"I don't think I want to stick around and quiz them," said Julie breathlessly.

"Me, either!" said Keeah. "Keep moving!"

They ran as quickly as they could, stopping only when they reached the bank of a wildly rushing river.

Eric scanned the white-capped waves. "It looks pretty dangerous. Should we cross?"

Khan shook his head. "No, no. I get soggy in water. Besides, crossing now would only slow us down. The riders would catch us."

Keeah nodded. "Khan's right. Let's hide here. If they cross, we'll double back to the castle."

Eric admired Keeah's ability to take control. He was glad she was there.

They ran along the bank until they came to a thicket of fruit trees. They huddled beneath them and waited.

The pounding hooves slowed. Animal feet stomped and dug at the ground. There was the strong smell of dirt churning underfoot and low voices murmuring to one another nearby.

Keeah grasped Eric's arm. Her eyes grew wide as she looked over his shoulder. "The ghost riders," she whispered. "They're right here."

"But I don't see them." He turned his head.

"No!" she said. "Don't look at them! No one look at them. I just remembered what Galen once told me. They aren't there till you look at them."

Khan's brow wrinkled. "Say that again?"

"They're ghosts," said Keeah. "They

make all kinds of noise chasing you, but they become visible only when you look in their eyes. Then they take an awful shape. And become dangerous."

"Oh, ugly dangerous ghosts," grumbled Neal, making himself as small as possible. "My favorite. All in all, I'd rather be eating toast."

"I agree," whispered Khan. "With thick gizzleberry jam, shared with my wife and children —"

"Shhh, you two," said Julie. "Listen!"

There was a sharp hissing sound to their right. It was answered by another on their left. A third whisper seemed to come from inches away. All of a sudden, the ghosts went silent, as if now they were listening for something.

A moment later, they all heard what it was.

Clip-clop! Clip-clop! Clip-clop!

"A pilka," whispered Julie, her eyes still shut.

Then, a squeaky voice broke into song.

Snibble-ibble-floot-boot!
The world is upside down.
A birdy wears a spider suit.
The wizard is a clown!

The voice was high-pitched and odd, but familiar. Eric opened one eye and caught sight of the pilka. On its back was a tall figure draped in a blue wizard's cloak. Eric couldn't see the figure's face, but he knew who it was.

After all, there was only one person who wore slippers on his hands and gloves on his feet, and rode facing backward on a pilka's saddle.

"It's Nelag!" he whispered.

Nelag was a pretend wizard Galen created to take his place when he was away. Even though he looked very much like Galen, Nelag had no real power, did everything backward, and was the exact opposite of the real Galen.

Even down to the spelling of his name.

The ghosts hissed in short, stabbing sounds.

"Nelag doesn't know about the riders," Neal whispered. "He'll hear them and look at them, and they'll pounce on him!"

"No they won't. I won't let them," said Keeah.

Eric trembled. "Keeah, wait —"

Clamping his eyes shut, Eric tried to hold Keeah back but grabbed Khan instead. This threw him off balance, and he fell backward into Julie.

The ghost riders' animals whinnied loudly.

The pretend wizard began to turn.

"Good-bye, whoever is there. How terrible to see you!"

"Don't look!" Keeah cried, leaping up.

"If you insist — I will!"

Keeah jumped toward Nelag. "I really mean *don't look!* No one look — no — one —"

"Get them now!" yelled one ghost.

Twigs crackled, branches split. Someone fell to the dirt with a thud, and someone else tumbled across the leaves.

Nelag shouted, "This is very nice!"

Keeah gave out a muffled cry.

Eric stood up to go after her, but stumbled on a tree root.

"Keep going, everyone!" cried Keeah, suddenly more distant. "Find the ship! I will see you — later!"

There came a strange shriek from the ghosts' animals, and an explosion of sparks.

Khan jostled Eric. "Come! We must do

as our princess says — run! With our eyes to the ground!"

They lurched to their feet and started to run to the river. Rushing ahead, Eric could hear Keeah fighting with blast after blast of her powerful magic.

A moment later, Khan stopped short, holding everyone back. "Oh, no. A waterfall!"

Looking up, they saw the river coiling wildly and plunging suddenly downward.

Neal glanced back around. "What about Nelag? Did they get him?"

"I heard him shouting, but I don't know," said Julie. "Neal, don't look back — wait — ahhhh!"

The slippery bank gave way beneath her.

Splurshhh! Julie fell into the water and was drawn instantly toward the waterfall.

"Help!"

Reaching for her, Khan also fell in. *Splish!*

Hooves beat the ground behind them again.

"Oh, man!" cried Eric, scrambling along the bank to the waterfall. "This can't be happening."

"Tell that to the ghosts!" said Neal.

The tramping hooves splashed into the water.

Julie cried out once more when the river dragged her over the falls. Khan squealed as he went over, too.

"We've got to follow our friends," said Eric.

Neal nodded. "Together, then."

With the ghost riders splashing closer, Eric and Neal leaped into the glistening, churning, ice-cold water.

Five

Surprise by Candlelight

The raging river pushed and pulled at the four friends, hurling them roughly down the falls, and into a bubbling pool at the bottom.

Splursh-sh-sh-shhhh!

"Aim for the — *blub!* — shore!" cried Julie, bobbing up and gasping for breath.

Khan's thin arms flailed wildly at the water to keep afloat. "Someone — grab my tassels!"

With all his might, Eric pushed across the water, grabbed Khan, and pulled him ashore.

Neal paddled and splashed and finally dragged himself up with the others next to the roaring waterfall.

For a while, no one said anything.

Then, even over the water's roar, they heard the stomping of heavy hooves.

"Those guys just don't give up!" growled Eric.

"Quickly," said Julie. "Behind the waterfall."

They darted behind the wall of rushing water and into a small cave inside. Holding their breath, they listened as the ghosts galloped down the riverbank and away.

Julie unfolded the map and shook the water from it. "They're going south along this river," she said, pointing to a thin blue line near the castle.

"It doesn't matter," said Eric. "We lost Keeah. We lost Nelag. We're supposed to be following Salamandra and Thog, but we lost them, too!"

"Keeah is a princess of great power," said Khan, shaking dry. "She will fight back."

"How do *we* fight back?" asked Neal, peeling off his socks. "We don't even know where Salamandra is."

Tap . . . tap.

"Hush!" Khan raised a finger to his lips.

Tap . . . tap . . . tap . . .

Julie squinted into the cave. "I see a tunnel. The sound is coming from there."

Carefully, the four soggy friends picked their way into the tunnel. They wandered this way and that until they saw a dull glow shimmering off the rough walls.

"A fire," said Khan, sniffing with each tiny step. "But what else shall we find?"

"Or who else?" Eric wondered aloud.

Stepping quietly around the last bend in the tunnel, they saw a small candle sitting on the rough floor. In its glow was a little creature, whose fur was dotted with red and yellow spots. It had bright eyes, a big snout, and short arms with long, delicate fingers.

In one paw it held a tiny silver hammer. In the other was a piece of shiny metal.

The creature before them was an imp.

An imp . . . they knew.

"Hob!" whispered Julie. "It's Hob!"

After each tap-tap-tap, the imp turned the metal in the candlelight, saying, "Hob, Hob, does a good job. Making a mask is a happy task!"

Hob was a great artist who once created a terrifying mask of power for the evil sorcerer, Lord Sparr. Hob had disappeared before he was caught.

Eric stepped forward. "Hob?"

The imp stopped tapping. He turned slowly.

"Children? Hob remembers you! And welcomes you, unless you have come to capture him. Then you shall see Hob scamper away!"

"Oh, no you don't!" said Khan, blocking the tunnel. "I've heard about the mischief you cause. Helping Lord Sparr? You, sir, are one bad imp!"

Hob hung his head, even as his eyes twinkled. "Some choose evil. Some don't. Hob did what he had to, then escaped from Sparr. Hee-hee! Escaped from those ghosts, too, with their ugly faces —"

Julie gasped. "Ghost riders? You *saw* them?"

Hob nodded. "I spied them in the forest."

"But how could you see the ghost riders and not be captured?" asked Eric.

The imp grinned. "Hob has . . . a secret —"

"Which Hob will share, if he knows what's good for him," said Khan, glaring at the imp.

"Very well . . ." Hob tugged lightly on his chin, then held out his hand. Glinting in the light of the candle was a mask hammered so thinly and delicately, it was nearly invisible.

"Hob's finest work so far," the imp said gleefully. "Just as the ghosts are invisible until you look in their eyes, in this mask Hob was invisible to them! It was so easy to escape from them!"

"Or maybe," said Eric, "to fight them."

Julie touched the mask. "And . . . just maybe . . . Salamandra herself?"

Hob grinned. "If you mean that creature with the tangled hair, it's true! Hob saw her. She tried to read his thoughts. But couldn't!"

The children stared at one another.

"This is awesome!" said Neal. "Masks like this would keep us from getting caught by the riders *and* nasty Miss Thornhead."

"We could find Keeah and stop Salamandra from flying Ko's dragon ship," said Eric. "Hob, I think we need masks for all of us."

"A job for Hob? Yes, yes, yes!" At once, the imp set to work, measuring the faces of the children, then tapping furiously with his hammer.

Eric's mask was completed first.

"Cool it in the falls before trying it," said Hob.

As the imp began Khan's mask and Neal and Julie looked at the book Thog had given her, Eric wormed his way back through the tunnels.

He held the mask under the water, shook it dry, and slipped it on. It felt as if

he had no mask on at all. He stepped out from the falls and onto the rocks.

The river glistened in the sunlight.

"Beautiful day," he said to himself. "Maybe it will turn out okay. Maybe we'll find Keeah —"

Crack! There was a sound from across the river. Eric jumped behind the waterfall and peered out.

A dozen gray animals, like horses, but covered with spikes, loped along the opposite bank.

On their backs rode . . . skeletons. Skeletons with ragged black cloaks pulled over their backs. Their eyes flashed with a sickly green color as they peered this way and that.

"Ghost riders . . ." Eric whispered.

In the middle of the pack, he caught sight of Keeah, tied onto a black saddle. She was struggling against the bonds, but could not break free.

His heart racing, Eric stepped out from behind the waterfall. He stood in plain sight, hoping Keeah would see him.

"They're hiding somewhere," hissed one of the riders, scanning the rocks where Eric stood.

So Hob is right. They can't see me! Eric thought.

"Never mind!" snorted another. "We've searched too long. We must begin our journey!"

As the riders speeded up, Keeah turned, stiffening in her saddle when she saw Eric.

She spoke silently to him.

Don't worry about me, she said. *Salamandra is the one. She's going to the island of Morka. Stop her!*

A hollow laugh rose from the bony creatures as their beasts trotted off into the woods.

Keeah! Eric called out silently to her.

She did not answer.

Breathlessly, he ran back through the tunnel, skidding into Hob's cave. "I just saw the ghost riders! Keeah, too. She's okay. Nelag wasn't there. But we have to get going. We have to!"

Eric felt strange taking command, but he knew Keeah wanted him to. He knew he had to.

"Put on your masks, everyone," he said. "We're on a mission to stop Salamandra!"

The imp jumped. "Hob will come, too. Neal's mask is not done. Hob will finish it as we go!"

Neal slipped it on and tried to line up the nose holes with his nostrils. "It does sort of pinch."

"Good enough," said Eric.

Finding Morka on the map and recalling the words he'd once heard Keeah use, he decided to try a transport spell.

"In a circle, everyone. Now, volo-bolo-sleeee!"

A silver light began to swirl around them.

"How wonderful!" said Khan excitedly.

"First stop — the island of Morka," said Eric. "And — here — we — goooooo!"

A moment later, they shot out of the cave, into the air, and up, up, and away over the lands of Droon.

Six

Island of Secrets

The spiral of light spun swiftly, carrying the three kids, the Lumpy king, and the mask-making imp over rivers, plains, and mountains.

"Um, Eric, should we be *wobbling* so much?" asked Julie, holding tight to Khan and Hob.

"I'm pretty sure that's normal," said Eric.

Neal looked down. "We're over water now."

"The S-s-sea . . . of . . . Droon," said Khan, his voice quavering as the light sputtered around him. "It is very d-d-deep . . . and very w-w-wet."

Eric pointed down through the light. "If my spell is working, that dot down there is Morka. Not bad for my first time using this spell, eh?"

Julie grimaced. "It might be your last time if you don't pull us up. We're dropping fast!"

Eric frowned. "I don't know how-ow-ow —"

The island seemed to zoom up at them, and — *wham! thwunk! splash-sh-sh-sh!* — they crash-landed on the tiny shore, rolling over and over on the beach and ending in a sandy heap.

Fzz-zz-zz-pop! The last of the sparks vanished.

Eric sat up, looked around at his friends, and laughed. "Was that awesome or what?"

Julie managed a smile. "I just hope we really are on the island of Morka. I couldn't take another *flight* right now. If that's what you call it."

"It's Morka," said Hob, looking around. "Hob once spent time here escaping from Lord Sparr."

Morka was home to the hog elves — chubby, pink, and mostly harmless creatures. The kids had met their king, Gryndal, once before.

Khan snorted. "Gryndal stole my crown a while back. I don't know if I can forget that!"

Julie scanned the steep hill rising over

the island. "I spy a village. Should we check it out?"

"I think so," said Eric. "Masks on firmly, everyone, and let's go."

"Mine still pinches," said Neal, starting up the hill after Eric. "But after a trip like that, I guess I'm happy to be alive!"

Winding paths crisscrossed what proved to be more a mountain than a steep hill. After nearly an hour, they came to a quiet village of huts.

"It looks fairly deserted," said Julie.

Hob shivered suddenly. "Not quite. Look!"

Huddled on a dusty street corner was . . .

"A monster!" the imp whispered.

It had scaly green skin and a spiky tail coiled in the dust. Sharp horns stuck out of its head.

Slowly, Eric stepped closer.

That was when the monster lifted its head.

Completely off.

With one of its hands — *ploink!* — the creature plucked its head up as if it were a helmet. Underneath was the chubby pink face and stubby three-nostriled snout of a hog elf.

Eric laughed. "It's Gryndal! King of the elves!"

The hog elf looked up sadly. "King? Humpf! My people have a new ruler now. That terrible Salamandra has taken over their minds!"

"She's here already?" said Julie.

Gryndal nodded. "Right now that wicked princess and her giant friend are digging in our mountain. And my own elves are helping! For some reason my monster mask saved me."

"Hob discovered that trick, too!" said the imp.

Eric looked up the mountainside. "We're here to stop Salamandra. You can help us."

"Help you?" he said, getting to his feet. "You have to help *me*! If they dig too deep, they'll hit our underground lake. We'll all be flooded!"

"What if we help one another?" said Julie.

Gryndal jumped. "Would you do that?"

Khan glared fiercely at the elf king. "You did steal my crown once. But that seems long ago. And a hog elf in trouble is . . . well . . . still in trouble. Yes, let's work together. And quickly, too!"

Plopping his mask back on, Gryndal led the small band up the mountain paths. Even before they reached the top, they saw the green beams of Salamandra's magic staff coloring the air.

Thwump! Boom-oom!

They peered over the jagged summit to see Thog digging giant boulders out of the mountain peak and stacking them aside. Standing at attention nearby were rows of chubby pink hog elves.

Gryndal snorted angrily. "See what she's done, that wicked princess with horrible hair?"

"Oh, she's not so bad. . . ." said Neal.

Everyone turned to see Neal, his mask lifted up and his eyes rolling slightly.

"Neal, are you nuts?" said Julie. "Your mask!"

"Huh? Oh, sorry," he said, slipping the mask back on. "It's just a little itchy under here."

"Shhh!" said Khan. "Look!"

Thog had suddenly stopped digging.

At once there came a strange groaning sound from the mountain's depths.

Eric shuddered. "Can anyone see any-thing?"

Khan peered up as high as he could, but shook his head. "Something old. I can smell that much!"

Salamandra spoke. "Bring them up, big boy!"

The green light still glazing his eyes, Thog grasped two objects nearly as large as himself.

They were flat and rounded at one end and tapered to a point at the other.

"They're . . . they're . . . wings," whis-pered Neal. "Big old dragon wings — made of metal!"

The wings were very large and clearly made of metal, but the odd, twisting de-signs hammered into them made them seem almost alive.

Hob shivered. "Hob knows those dark

symbols. They are from Ko's ancient empire of Goll!"

It was only then that Eric began to understand the powerful evil of Ko's ancient ship.

"Thog said the real danger was where the ship flies to," he murmured to his friends. "Wherever that is, we can't let Salamandra get there."

"We must act quickly," whispered Gryndal, pointing to a small hole near Thog's feet. It was bubbling with water. "Our underground lake won't be underground much longer."

"Then, let's do it," said Eric. Jumping up, he cried, "Salamandra! We're here to stop you —"

"We're *all* here to stop you," said Julie, standing together with Neal, Hob, Khan, and Gryndal.

Salamandra wheeled around, staring into their eyes. "What a cute little army! I see you're all wearing masks, too. How clever. Still, the dragon ship will fly — and I will rule Droon!"

Kla-boom! She sent a bolt of green lightning at Eric. He dodged the blast, swung around, and shot back at her. *Wump!* A chunk of watery dirt blew up, splattering her with mud.

Julie laughed. "Actually, that looks good on you! Are you ready for your mud bath?"

With Neal and Khan on one side and Hob and Gryndal on the other, they hurled rocks into the gathering mud puddles, splattering the thorn princess.

Angrily waving her staff around, Salamandra sent a huge blast at the ground.

Kla-booooom! Water gushed from the depths in huge spurts.

Laughing, the wicked princess turned again to the children. "I hope you enjoyed your little fight. Our real battle hasn't even begun. Thog — come. In two minutes, this little island will fall right into the sea!"

With that, she twirled her staff three times and she and the giant vanished into thin air.

No longer under Salamandra's spell, the hog elves went scurrying for cover. An instant later, a huge wall of water exploded from the mountaintop and thundered down toward the elves' tiny village.

Seven

The Puzzle of the Past

The water gushed down into a narrow pass above the village, threatening to crash through and sweep the village away.

"Somebody do something!" cried Gryndal, jumping up and down.

Eric turned to Julie. "Fly me to Thog's pile of boulders. Then help everyone get out of the way."

"You got it!" said Julie. Taking Eric's

hand, she shot to the rock pile, then flew back to help move the elves to safety.

Staring up at the huge boulders, Eric closed his eyes and summoned up some magic words.

"Nomee-akwee-petree!"

A blast of blue sparks burst from his fingertips and struck the tower of rocks.

Rmm-blam-boom! A boulder rolled off the top and tumbled onto the pass below. *Splash!*

"And again!" he said to himself. Another blast, and another boulder rolled from the pile. Then another. And another. Finally, the entire pile Thog had dug up went crashing onto the pass.

Rmmm-fwoosh-ppkkshh! The rushing water struck the wall of boulders, curled high, then rolled back on itself.

The village was safe.

"Yee-bo-yee! Plit-plit-plit!" the elves cheered.

So did Neal. "Woo-hoo! You did it!"

Gryndal rushed to Julie and Eric. "How can I ever thank you? You have saved our village!"

But Eric's thoughts had returned to Salamandra. He shook his head. "We lost her. She's already across the sea."

Gryndal smiled. "This isn't over yet. Salamandra stole some old wings, but we have other wings to offer you. Come, come!"

The king and his hog elves scurried beyond the village to a field where two giant birds were grazing. Two birds . . . with four wings each.

"Soarwings!" said Julie. "I remember them!"

They all remembered how Keeah had once flown away on a soarwing in search of her mother.

"Climb on," said Gryndal. "Find Keeah. Stop the wicked thorn princess. Save Droon!"

"Thanks for all you've done," said Eric, climbing with his friends onto the backs of the birds.

"No, thank *you*!" cheered the hog elves.

At once the giant birds lifted, circled the tiny island, and soared up to the wispy pink clouds.

They flew swiftly across the ocean. In what seemed like no time the children were over the coast.

"Where do you think Salamandra has gone?" asked Julie, peering down through the clouds. "Droon is huge. She could be anywhere."

"Not far, I suspect," said Khan, sniffing the air.

Eric shrugged. "We'll just have to search until . . . until . . . holy cow!"

Dipping below the clouds, they saw the shimmering towers of Jaffa City. And inside the city walls, crossing the main courtyard, were Thog and the wicked princess herself.

"This can't be good," said Hob.

"That's not the worst of it," said Neal. "Look."

They saw King Zello, Keeah's large, club-carrying Viking of a father, standing in a swirl of green light, frozen to the palace stairs. Next to him was Queen Relna, Keeah's wizard mother.

"Salamandra put her charm on them, too," said Khan. "I knew I sniffed danger."

"I can't sniff at all," said Neal. "My mask really pinches my nose. Hob, could you please . . . ?"

"Oh, all right!" said the imp, taking the mask. "But keep your head down and don't peek!"

The giant birds skimmed the ground, and the kids slid off their wings one by one, tumbling onto the soft grass outside the walls. A moment later, the birds soared into the clouds again.

Being careful to keep out of sight, the small band made its way into the city's main square.

"Salamandra's been busy," said Julie, pointing.

Strapped on Thog's back were the two gleaming wings, a jeweled ship's wheel, and a large dragon's head formed of bronze.

Eric shuddered. "Wow. She's almost finished collecting the pieces of the ship."

"What's happening?" asked Neal, his eyes shut tight. "Can I look?"

"Not until your mask is done," said Hob, quietly tapping the metal.

Before they knew it, Thog went to the royal stables, shooed some pilkas away, and began digging a long trench under the stalls.

The kids crept along the city wall, then darted behind a high pile of hay and peeked over.

When they did, they saw Thog pull a giant silver hull up out of the dirt. It was formed like a dragon's body. Its scaly sides glinted in the sun.

"And now . . . the final piece!" said Salamandra, her eyes scanning the paper stolen from Galen's tower. She pointed past the stables. "Thog, find the sail of my dragon ship!"

The green light still swimming in his eyes, Thog stomped like a robot to the main square. Reaching up, he tugged the city's giant flagpole up out of the ground. *Ploink!* The large blue flag drooped and dragged across the ground.

"Oh!" said Khan, burying his head in

his hands. "The noble flag of Droon! I cannot look!"

"Look?" said Neal. "Look at what? What's going on?" He lifted his head.

"Don't look at anything!" said Hob, still tapping. "I haven't quite finished —"

Neal's eyes opened just long enough for Salamandra's green light to flash in them.

"Oww! Whoa! Huh?" he mumbled. "Yes, princess. Of course, princess. You bet!"

He stumbled toward her, murmuring softly.

Eric turned. "Neal? Neal! Get back here —"

"Droon, prepare to be mine," cried Salamandra. "Shadowthorn will live again. When I fly this ship, there will be no stopping me!"

"Shadowthorn sounds nice," mumbled

Neal, his eyes rolling. "Can I get a room with a view?"

Laughing, Salamandra waved her hand. "Thog, come. We have one more stop!"

The giant stuffed the flagpole into his bundle, picked up Salamandra, and carried her away over the walls.

Neal started after them, but Eric and Julie held him down while Hob slapped the mask on him.

"You're staying with us," said Eric.

Neal blinked "Huh? What? Oh, man. Thanks, guys. I glanced at her ugly staff, everything went green, and — *boom!* — my mind was gonzo."

"Now that's a scary thought," said Julie.

"It *was* scary!" said Neal. "Especially when she started telling stuff to my brain. I forget most of it, but I did learn Salamandra's next stop."

Eric gulped. "Some place not good?"

"Some place *very* not good," said Neal, taking the map and tapping his finger on a black spot. "She's going . . . are you ready? . . . to Plud."

"Plud!" Khan said with a gasp. "Lord Sparr's terribly creepy castle in the Dark Lands?"

"Where all of Sparr's chubby red Ninn warriors live?" asked Julie.

"The Forbidden City of Plud?" asked Hob.

"Plud the wicked? Plud the evil?" asked Eric.

"That's the place," said Neal. "Sorry."

"But I thought Plud burned down," said Eric. "Why would Salamandra go there?"

"We can tell you why," boomed a loud voice.

The kids turned to see King Zello, free of Salamandra's spell, running across the square toward them. Queen Relna was running right next to him.

Everyone bowed to them.

"If Salamandra is going to Plud," said Relna, "it is because the highest tower remains . . . and the weapons workshop."

King Zello nodded his head. "Whatever else they are, Ninns are builders of things. Weapons mostly, but anything in metal."

"That's it!" said Eric. "Salamandra needs to rebuild the ship. And Plud is the one place that has the workers and the tools."

"She's got everything she needs!" said Julie.

"There is one thing more she needs," said Queen Relna. "Long ago, Galen discovered — as Salamandra soon will — a secret about the dragon ship.

"A secret?" asked Khan.

The queen nodded. "Only a wizard's

power can make Ko's ship fly. Lightning shall strike, the ship shall rise, and the wizard's power will be drained away . . . forever."

The children went silent.

Neal's eyes got huge. "Uh-oh. I just remembered another thing Salamandra said."

"What?" asked Eric.

"Keeah is in Plud, too."

Eight

Zello's Believe It or Not

Standing in the flagless square of Jaffa City, Relna turned to the king. "I will free Galen and Max as quickly as I can, then come to Plud."

Eric's heart raced. "We'll rescue Keeah and stop Salamandra. We have to."

"And we will," said Julie firmly.

Eric nodded. He only hoped they'd be in time.

As the queen sped off to the wizard's

tower, King Zello called his guards. A moment later, they brought a giant, multi-colored balloon. It had a large basket underneath, with shiny pipes on each side.

"Cool!" said Neal. "It looks jet powered."

Zello beamed. "Friddle the inventor made it. It goes very fast. And we need speed. Pile in!"

With a roar of flame, the balloon shot into the air. At once Zello set a course for Plud, while Hob set to work making him a mask.

"We must stop that ship," the king murmured under his breath. "We simply must."

Julie nudged Eric. "Go ahead. You ask."

Eric frowned. "Um, King Zello, do you know where the dragon ship flies to?"

The king stroked his golden beard, then sighed. "I will tell you what I know, even though parts of the story are hard to believe."

As the balloon sped over the plains and hills below, he began. "You know that Emperor Ko was a sorcerer of great power. His empire of Goll spread evil over half of Droon. And yet, in his younger days, Galen was able to defeat him."

"Galen was very cool," said Neal. "He still is."

"Cool, indeed," said the king. "But, this is the part of the legend that's hard to believe. It says that when Ko came near to death, the dragon ship flew him to his birthplace, the source of his dark power."

"Where is that?" asked Julie.

"Beyond the Serpent Sea, on the Isle of Mists, a place so old it doesn't appear on any map."

Khan quivered on his feet. His eyes grew big.

"What happened there?" asked Eric.

The king frowned. "Here the legend has nothing to say, and we are left to wonder. I will only say that Ko's body has never been found. If his birthplace does exist, not even Salamandra will be prepared for what she finds there."

The balloon dipped into thick, smoky air. The ragged ground beneath them was charred black.

"Welcome to the Dark Lands," said Neal. "There's just nothing like them."

"Thank goodness for that!" said Hob, handing the king his completed mask. "You'll need this."

Within moments, they saw the forbidden city itself, a mass of black stone, its one surviving tower jutting up through the air like a dead tree.

Eric thought of the army of large, red-faced Ninn warriors that filled Plud's dark hallways. "It's the home of evil," he murmured.

"And total opposite of Jaffa City," said Julie.

Zello pulled a cord, and the balloon landed gently on the shore of Plud's frozen lake.

The smell of burning wood filled the air.

"I know that smell," said Khan. "The Ninns are heating their furnace. Soon we'll hear —"

Clank! Klong! Pling!

"The sound of hammers," said Neal. "It's like when my dad fixes stuff at home. Well, he tries. It usually doesn't work after he fixes it."

"Well, we'll fix Salamandra!" said Zello. He pulled an enormous wooden club out of the balloon and gave it a pat. "Eric, Julie, Neal, go with Khan and Hob to where the

Ninns are rebuilding the ship. Do what you can to stop them."

"Where will you go?" asked Julie.

"To find Keeah," he said, scampering off. "And I'll whup any Ninns who try to stop me!"

Silently and carefully, the children, Khan, and Hob wormed their way through the burned walls and out into the vast courtyard. The giant, Thog, lay inside, sleeping with his back against the wall.

"All he wanted was to read books," said Neal.

"I hope he will be able to again soon," said Khan, sniffling. "As I hope to read to my children soon."

Eric put his hand on the Lumpy's shoulder. "You will. We'll get out of here. Keeah, too."

Khan sniffed up his tears. "Quite right!"

The sound of heavy hammers banging

and crashing drew them to the deepest chamber of the fortress, where the Ninns' workshop was.

The black room blazed with light. Giant flames leaped from a large pit against the back wall. On a round stone platform beside it stood the flying ship, glimmering in the flame light.

Eric shivered with fear.

The ship's sleek wings jutted out from the scaly silver hull. On the front stood the figurehead of the dragon, its fangs as sharp as daggers.

"That thing is pretty scary," whispered Neal.

"The scary part is that we're too late," said Julie.

Using ropes and pulleys, one group of red-faced Ninns hoisted the flagpole onto the deck and another group hammered it into place.

Then, giving a gargily shout, the Ninns stood back as the platform slowly began to rise. The ceiling opened up, and the ship passed into the room above. Its ceiling was opening, too.

"The ship is going to the top of the tower," said Eric. "I bet that's where Salamandra is."

"Let's get up there," said Khan. "Now!"

As they rushed up through the tower, they heard the crackling boom of lightning overhead.

"Didn't Keeah's mom say that you need lightning to transfer power to the ship?" asked Neal.

"Salamandra's conjuring a storm," said Julie.

Ka-boooom! The tower walls shook.

Hob squealed. "A lightning storm? With thunder? Hob doesn't like lightning. Hob must flee!"

With that, he leaped away down the stairs.

"Wait! Hob, stop!" Julie called. "Oh, I'll get him. You guys keep going to the roof. Hob!"

As she ran off after the imp, Neal, Eric, and Khan looked at one another grimly.

"We started this mission with a whole lot more people than we have now," said Neal.

"I noticed that," said Eric. "No Keeah, no King Zello, no Hob, no Julie. How about we make a pact? The three of us have to stay together, okay?"

"Real together," said Neal. "Like triplets."

Khan smiled. "After all, we are like family. Now, come. Let us do what needs to be done!"

They raced step-by-step, floor by floor, up through the tower. As they approached the summit, they began to hear the sounds of a vicious fight — *clank! whumpf! blonk!*

The three friends burst onto the tower's roof at the exact moment that Keeah herself, her golden hair flying, blasted a gang of bony ghost riders.

"You can't keep me tied up!" she snarled.

Eric felt his heart leap. "Yes! You're free!"

"Just barely!" she said, shooting Eric a smile. She swung her father's wooden club at two ghost riders, sending them reeling back down the stairs. "Daddy, behind you — catch!"

The king whirled around, caught the club, and sent another three ghosts crashing backward.

"Get the ghosts. They can't see us!" Eric shouted. He jumped into the fight, shooting blast after blast of blue sparks from his fingertips.

Between them, Khan and Neal tripped three ghosts who crashed sideways into four others.

Keeah and Zello charged another band that came climbing up over the walls.

The fight was fierce. But it didn't last long.

In a puff of foul-smelling smoke, Salamandra appeared on the tower and thrust her staff high.

Ka-booom! A huge blast shook the tower.

Neal flew back into Eric and Khan. All three went tumbling behind a broken section of wall.

Groggily, Eric peered over the jagged stones.

King Zello was in a heap, his head raised to look at Salamandra. His mask sat glinting on the ground. His eyes were rolling slowly in his head.

Keeah struggled to get up, but a troop of Ninns charged from behind and surrounded her.

Salamandra sauntered over and stood staring at her. "So . . . here we are, princess to princess!"

"You don't deserve the title," said Keeah, struggling. "And you'll never be queen, either. My mother is the only queen of Droon. And right now, she's setting Galen free of your wicked spell. He'll be here soon —"

"Not soon enough," Salamandra interrupted. "I should have captured the old wizard when I had the chance. But if the ship needs power to make it fly, I suppose you'll do. Look, it begins!"

Grrr-vrrrrt. Part of the floor spiraled open and the dragon ship rose up from below, turning slowly on its stone platform.

The ship was as sleek and swift-looking as the most powerful ship of the sea, and Eric shuddered to think that Salamandra just might fly it.

To Ko's legendary Isle of Mists.

With a nod, Salamandra commanded the Ninns to tie Keeah onto a sort of pedestal on the ship's deck. "I have a long way to go, princess. I only hope you are powerful enough."

"Let me go and you'll see how powerful I am!" Keeah said, even as she was strapped in.

"We have to help her," Eric whispered.

"I'll help you," said Khan firmly. "And so will Neal. Isn't that right, Neal?"

Neal breathed in deeply. "I didn't like it when Crazy Hair took over my mind. I'll do anything to keep her from messing with it again. I might need it someday."

Eric gave his friends a smile. "Okay, then, here's my plan. . . ."

But even as he told them, Salamandra howled at the sky, and bolt after bolt of jagged lightning exploded over Plud's black tower.

Nine

A Very Important Person

Kkk — boom-oom! Lightning crashed everywhere at once, turning the black sky white.

"That's your plan?" said Neal when Eric had finished. "Run fast and save Keeah from getting fried?"

Eric nodded. "Except instead of running fast, I said we should run *really* fast!"

"Still," said Khan, "it's not very . . . plannish."

"Did I mention the distraction?" asked Eric.

Neal's eyes lit up. "Did you say . . . *distraction*? Whoa, am I the guy for that!"

Neal whispered briefly in Khan's ear.

The Lumpy king smiled. "I can do that!"

"Then what are we waiting for?" said Eric. "One, two, three — go!"

At Eric's signal, Neal and Khan jumped up and started to run, screaming at the top of their lungs. "Blaga-blaga-yee-yee-yee! Go-team-go!"

"What?" said Salamandra, turning to them.

At the same time, Eric leaped for the ship, his fingers raised and sparking wildly. "Keeah, get ready to move —"

All of a sudden, a voice cried out. "STOP!"

Everyone — the Ninns, the ghost riders, the children, even Salamandra herself — stopped what they were doing and turned to the tower stairs.

There stood a small, spotted creature. Hob.

The grin on his face stretched from one fuzzy ear to the other.

"What is he doing?" asked Khan, tiptoeing up to Eric and Neal. The two boys shook their heads.

Salamandra sneered, even as the lightning continued to crackle overhead. "You silly little imp — you are not needed here. Be gone!"

Hob held up his hand. "Hob has a question for Salamandra." He took two steps toward the sorceress, then stopped.

"I thought Hob was afraid of lightning," whispered Neal. "He must be up to something."

The imp went on. "Hob wonders why Salamandra wants to power her flying dragon ship with the small powers of a junior wizard . . . when she can have the greatest wizard of all."

The thorn princess narrowed her eyes at him. "What are you saying?"

"Hob is saying," the imp went on, stepping closer, "that instead of Princess Keeah, you could power your ship with . . . Galen himself!"

With that, Hob waved his arm in a flourish toward the tower stairs. A figure in a long blue robe, tall coned hat, white beard, and a sad face marked with age strode slowly up the stairs.

"Galen?" Eric gasped. "What . . . what?"

"It is I," said the wizard, looking sadly at Eric and the others. "Max, come."

A moment later, trembling and whim-

pering, the eight-legged figure of Max bounded up the stairs and took his place next to the wizard.

"Galen! Max!" cried Keeah. "Get away from here — now! Salamandra is too powerful!"

The next moment, a dozen stern-faced Ninns followed the wizard and the spider troll up the stairs, brandishing long swords.

"Captured!" said Salamandra, her eyes beaming with cruel delight. "Hob, you imp! What a clever idea!"

Eric stared at Hob. "How could you do this? I thought you were on our side! How could you turn on us like this?"

The little imp gave Eric a mischievous smile. "Hob knows where the real power is. Hob must look out for . . . Hob!"

The wizard turned to the children. "Alas, it is true. I am sorry to have put you in such danger."

"Queen Relna freed us from the tower," Max whimpered. "We were coming here to rescue Keeah, when Hob surprised us in the halls with this band of Ninns. We were caught off guard . . . and caught for real!"

Salamandra howled. "Yes! I achieve all my goals with one single act! The great wizard Galen loses his power, and I fly my ship all the way to the Isle of Mists. There I shall discover the greatest power Droon has ever known!"

She pointed her staff at the Ninns. "Make the switch! Give me . . . Galen!"

Swiftly, the Ninns released Keeah and strapped the old wizard onto the ship's pedestal.

Then, as she had before, Salamandra lifted her hand and — *flang!* — no one could move.

"And now!" Salamandra raised her staff high.

Kkkkk! Lightning struck the pedestal and the transfer of power began.

Everyone stood frozen to their places as a thick stream of blue light flowed from the wizard into the flying ship itself.

"Stop this!" said Eric. "Stop it!"

"No one can stop me," Salamandra snarled.

A moment went by. Then another.

Rr-rrr! Fwing! Fwing-g-g!

The giant wings flapped once . . . twice . . . and the ship began to rise from the platform.

"You see? See? Ko's dragon ship flies!" Salamandra howled as she leaped onto the deck. "To the Isle of Mists. To the greatest secret of ancient Droon. To my new power — forever!"

The ghost riders quickly piled onto the ship.

With great ceremony, Salamandra took

her place at the big, jeweled wheel. She turned it.

The giant golden wings fluttered more rapidly, and the ship lifted higher, circling the black tower of Plud.

As the children watched, bit by bit, all the light left the old wizard and entered the ship itself, which began to glow brightly.

Keeah gasped. "No . . . no . . . no . . ."

With a shudder of wings and a roar from its dragon figurehead, the ship rose up and away and into the sky.

"To the Isle of Mists!" Salamandra bellowed.

Her yellow eyes blazed with evil as the enchanted flying ship left the Dark Lands and set a course to the coast of the Serpent Sea and beyond . . . to the birthplace of Emperor Ko.

Ten

Follow That Ship!

Clank-ank-ank! As the big ship drove away, the spell was finally lifted, and the bewildered Ninns dropped their swords.

Eric raced over to Keeah. "Are you all right?"

"I'm fine!" she said, first seeing that her father was unhurt. "But someone won't be!"

She stomped over to the little imp.

"Hob!" she said angrily. "What have you done? How could you do this to

Galen? The first wizard of Droon! His powers are *gone!*"

The little imp tried to back up, but Eric, Neal, Khan, and King Zello surrounded him.

"What should we do with him?" said Khan.

"Wait!" said Max. "Before you do anything, I have something to show you. Watch!"

Everyone turned to the furry spider troll.

Suddenly, he began to twist and wiggle and shake and spin. A moment later — *ploink!* — the spider troll was no longer a spider troll.

Max had become . . .

"Julie!" cried Keeah. "But . . . wait . . . *Julie?*"

"The very same!" said Julie, blinking

her eyes and stretching her arms. "It was never Max. It was me all the time —"

"But how?" asked Eric, not quite believing his eyes. "How could you even *do* that?"

Julie laughed and pulled the small yellow book from the pocket of her shorts. "Remember the book Thog let me borrow? It has a page about the powers of wingwolves. We already knew they could fly, but they also have the ability to change shape —"

"I was right!" said Eric. "I told you you might have other powers!"

Julie grinned. "When Hob told me about his plan, I became Max!"

Keeah frowned. "But where is the real Max?"

"In the tower with the real Galen!" said Hob.

Eric glanced up at the flying ship that was fast disappearing over the horizon. "Then who did Salamandra just zap all the wizard power out of?"

At that, Hob did a little dance. "That, my friends, was none other than a certain *pretend* wizard named . . . Nelag!"

"Wait a second," said Zello. "Nelag is sort of . . . opposite. If the ship has his power, then —"

Vrrrrroom — eeeekkk! The flying ship wobbled sharply, spun almost completely around, and made a steep dive.

Hob jumped with glee. "It is Hob's clever plan at work. Salamandra is in big trouble now!"

"So is Nelag," said Khan. "Poor fellow!"

King Zello boomed out a laugh. "Poor Salamandra! There's only one way to catch a fast ship — with a faster one! Into the balloon, people! We're in a race!"

Hooting and hollering, the four children, Hob, Khan, and Zello dashed through the tower and leaped directly into the balloon's basket. Zello pushed on the controls, and the balloon shot off.

"After that dragon ship!" shouted Keeah.

Eric, Julie, Neal, and Keeah huddled together at the front of the basket as the balloon soared over the plains of Droon.

Keeah's hair flew wildly in the wind.

"I'm so glad you're safe," said Eric. "We all are. We were . . . scared."

"I was scared, too," she said. "But I knew you would help me if you could."

"Anytime," said Neal.

"Anywhere," said Julie.

"We're catching up," said Khan, saluting the king of Droon. "Permission to board, sir?"

"Permission granted!" boomed King Zello.

Even as Salamandra tried to control the swift flying ship, it dipped and wobbled, soared and dived. With each crazy motion, Nelag whooped delightedly, "I hate this! Oh, it's bad!"

"Meaning he loves it!" said Neal.

Moments later, the balloon pulled alongside the dragon ship. Together, the four children, Khan, and King Zello leaped on board.

"Get them!" Salamandra cried from the wheel.

"I don't think so," Keeah shot back. Tossing the ghost riders aside, she and her father charged the sorceress from one side, while Eric shot a blast of sparks from the other.

Blam! The thorn staff clattered to the deck and slid off the ship. It dropped right into the balloon below, where it landed at Hob's feet.

He held it up and cheered.

Neal cheered, too — "Wa-hoo!" — as he, Khan, and Julie freed Nelag from his place on the pedestal.

The sandy dunes of Lumpland were just coming into view when the ship took a steep dive.

"We're going down!" said King Zello. "Everyone back to the balloon — the good folks, I mean!"

With Julie's help, they flew back to the balloon. A few moments later, it landed gently on a dune next to Galen's thorn-covered tower.

"I will get you all!" Salamandra howled at them. "You haven't seen the last of me — ohhh!"

Vrrrroomm! The ship now began to spin around and around. At the same time there was a loud rumbling coming from the distance.

Thomp-thomp-thomp!

Suddenly, a giant appeared, leaping over the dunes, kicking up waves of sand.

"Thog!" cried Julie. "You're back!"

"I must save our flag!" the giant yelled.

As the ship lurched and jerked toward the dunes, Thog leaped up, grabbed the mast and sail with one hand, and pulled it loose — *ploink!*

"Hooray!" yelled Khan as the great flag of Droon waved once more.

Vooom! The ship jerked downward, engulfed entirely in blue light. There was a sudden popping sound, a flash of flame, and one final shriek from Salamandra. Then there was nothing. The sky was empty. They were gone. All of them.

The wicked princess. The creepy ghost riders. Ko's enchanted dragon ship.

All had vanished as if they had never existed.

"Where did they go?" asked Neal.

Zello shook his head. "I'm not sure, but perhaps Galen can tell us. He's about to be freed."

Keeah had already run to join her mother. Linking arms, the queen and her daughter sent a powerful stream of blue light at the tower.

Zzzzz-blam! The thorns fell away from the tower walls and seemed to vanish into nothing, just as Salamandra herself had disappeared.

The real Max and Galen scrambled down from the upper room as their friends hurried to them.

When he had heard the whole story, Galen scanned the sky above. "I doubt we will see her anytime soon," he said. "Good work, friends."

"Thank you all for saving our true princess!" said Max, hugging Keeah tightly.

"But, tell me, Nelag, how did you manage to convince everyone you were my real master?"

"I should like to know that, too," said Galen.

The pretend wizard turned completely around, scratched his feet, and chuckled. "I just spoke nonsense. It must have come out right!"

Galen himself laughed. "Hmm. Very funny."

"Very clever, too!" said Nelag, putting slippers on his hands. "It was I who sent the children a message through their soccer ball!"

Julie frowned, then laughed. "Of course. The message always comes backward. The ball said G-a-l-e-n — meaning — Nelag!"

"You're welcome," said Nelag, yawning.

"But how did you know Keeah needed your help at the tower?" asked King Zello.

"After the ghost riders captured Keeah, I followed them. Hob found me in the halls of Plud," said Nelag. "It was his plan."

"So," said Queen Relna, "we must thank little Hob for his clever plan to save Keeah. Good work, Hob. Hob? Now where has he gone to?"

Nelag laughed. "Why, Hob is right here!"

He pointed to the empty space next to him.

Julie's eyes went wide. "Which means that Hob is definitely missing again."

"Hob isn't the only thing missing," said Khan, peering into the balloon's basket. "Salamandra's magic staff is gone, too."

Keeah blinked. "Hob has the thorn staff?"

"If he does," said Galen, "then he's a

small imp with big power. We'll just have to find him."

"Can we come, too?" asked Eric.

"Of course," said Keeah. "We didn't have anything planned for tomorrow, anyway —"

There came a sudden whooshing sound.

"Look," said Thog, pointing. "It's beautiful!"

The rainbow-colored staircase stood shimmering over a nearby sand dune.

"Time to go," said Julie. She handed Thog the small yellow book. "Thank you. I learned a lot."

Thog bowed and bid everyone goodbye, saying he would plant the flag in Jaffa City then return to his home in Zorfendorf Castle. "To read a quiet book," he said.

As they watched the giant go, Neal turned to his friends. "Today has been pretty action-packed. And also pretty awesome."

"It's always awesome," said Keeah.

Then, while Keeah and her parents and Galen and Max headed to Khan's little home for supper, the three friends stepped onto the stairs.

Eric smiled. "You know, guys, today was one of the good days. One of the very good days."

"Let's hope there are lots more," said Julie.

Neal grinned. "And that was one wild ride."

"Let's hope there are lots more of those, too!" said Eric.

With a final wave to their friends in Droon, Eric, Julie, and Neal raced up the magic staircase for home.